Hush,
Baby
Ghostling

Hush, Baby Ghostling

by **Andrea Beaty**
and **Pascal Lemaitre**

Margaret K. McElderry Books
New York   London   Toronto   Sydney

Hush,

Baby Ghostling.

The **haunting hour** is past.

The bats have ceased their swooping and the dawn is coming fast.

So nestle safe beside me in our happy haunted home,

and dream a dream
of darkness
where the
wild monsters
roam.

Dear Baby Ghostling.
You're **tucked in** nice and tight.

I'll leave some
darkness in the hall
if you're scared of the light.

It's late, my dear.

The sun is near.

Just one **last lullaby**.

I'll wake you when the moon—

once more—

is shining in the sky.

Sweet Baby Ghostling.

What is that you hear?

Songs and laughter in your room?

It's just the wind, my dear.

Close your eyes and drift to sleep and

Of hisses, howls, and screeching owls.

dream of midnight skies.

Of bats and banshee cries.

Poor Baby Ghostling.

Mr. Bones is gone?

You think somebody stole him

when you closed your eyes to yawn?

Here he is, my darling—

sleeping safe beneath your bed.

Have no fear.

Just hold him near

and rest your sleepy head.

Yes, Baby Ghostling.

I'll turn the darkness on,

and I won't turn it off again

till all your fears are gone.

Now dream a little nightmare while

Dream a dream of darkness where

the ghoulies dance and sway.

the wild monsters play.

What, Baby Ghostling?

You've had another scare?

You've **seen a boy**

with ten pink toes, blue eyes,

and golden hair?

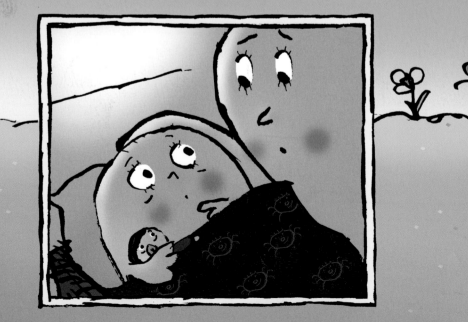

Of course I'll search your closet.

Every pocket.

Every sleeve.

But please don't fear the childlings, dear.

They're only

make-believe.

Hush,

Baby Ghostling.

I've nothing left to do
but hug and kiss you once again
and whisper . . .

"I love you."

To my spouseling and childlings with love
—A. B.

*To my beloved daughter, Maelle, and
her beloved mother, Manou*
—P. L.

Margaret K. McElderry Books
An imprint of Simon & Schuster Children's Publishing Division
1230 Avenue of the Americas, New York, New York 10020
Text copyright © 2009 by Andrea Beaty
Illustrations copyright © 2009 by Pascal Lemaitre
Book design by Ann Bobco
The text for this book is set in Fairplex.
The illustrations for this book are rendered in bamboo and ink, then digitally colored.
Manufactured in China
10 9 8 7 6 5 4 3 2 1
Library of Congress Cataloging-in-Publication Data
Beaty, Andrea.
Hush, Baby Ghostling / Andrea Beaty ; illustrated by Pascal Lemaitre.—1st ed.
p. cm.
Summary: At bedtime a mother ghost reassures her child that there is nothing to fear in
their haunted home, especially not humans, since they are make-believe.
ISBN-13: 978-1-4169-2545-3 (hardcover)
ISBN-10: 1-4169-2545-7 (hardcover)
[1. Bedtime—Fiction. 2. Ghosts—Fiction. 3. Mother and child—Fiction.
4. Monsters—Fiction.] I. Lemaitre, Pascal, ill. II. Title.
PZ8.3.B38447Hus 2009
[E]—dc22
2007047034

FIRST
EDITION